Hello, Hippo! Goodbye, Bird!

by
KRISTYN CROW

illustrated by
POLY BERNATENE

ALFRED A. KNOPF
New York

For the great Rick Walton, mentor and friend—K.C.

To Paula, together we make a great team!—P.B.

THIS IS A BORZOI BOOK PUBLISHED BY ALFRED A. KNOPF

Text copyright © 2016 by Kristyn Crow
Jacket art and interior illustrations copyright © 2016 by Poly Bernatene

Visit us on the Web! randomhousekids.com

Educators and librarians, for a variety of teaching tools, visit us at RHTeachersLibrarians.com

Library of Congress Cataloging-in-Publication Data
Crow, Kristyn, author.
Hello, hippo! goodbye, bird! / by Kristyn Crow ; [illustrated by Poly Bernatene]. — First edition.
pages cm.
Summary: A hippo and a bird become unlikely friends.
ISBN 978-0-553-50990-8 (trade) — ISBN 978-0-553-50991-5 (lib. bdg.) — ISBN 978-0-553-50992-2 (ebook)
1. Hippopotamus—Juvenile fiction. 2. Birds—Juvenile fiction. 3. Friendship—Juvenile fiction.
[1. Hippopotamus—Fiction. 2. Birds—Fiction. 3. Friendship—Fiction.] I. Bernatene, Poly, illustrator. II. Title.
PZ7.C885355He 2015   [E]—dc23   2014043817

The text of this book is set in Messipes, Elogy, Chinchilla, Blue Century, and Prater Sans.
The illustrations were created using mixed media, including pencils and digital color.

MANUFACTURED IN CHINA
April 2016
10 9 8 7 6 5 4 3 2 1

First Edition

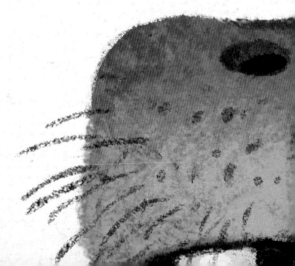

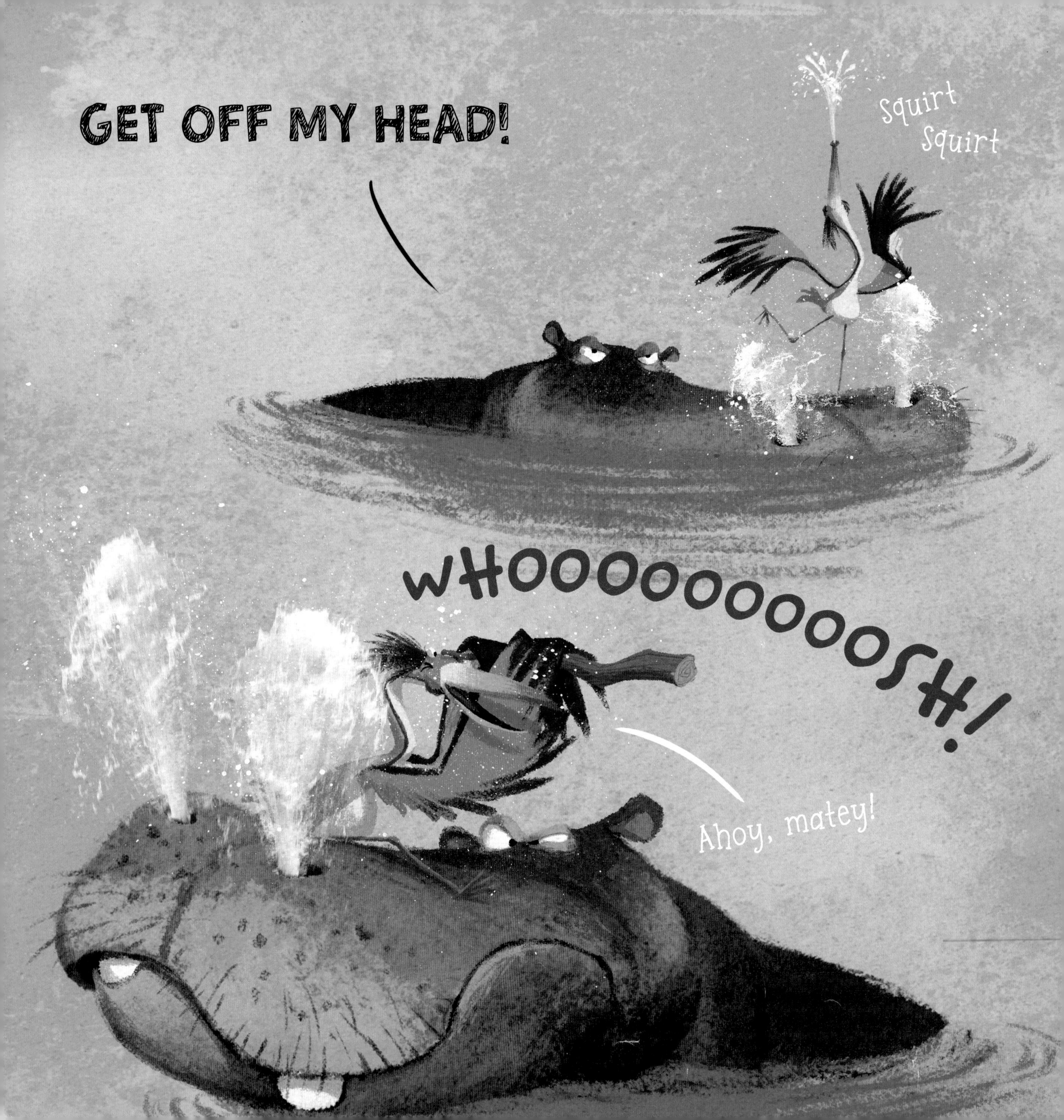
GET OFF MY HEAD!
Squirt
Squirt
WHOOOOOOOOOOOSH!
Ahoy, matey!

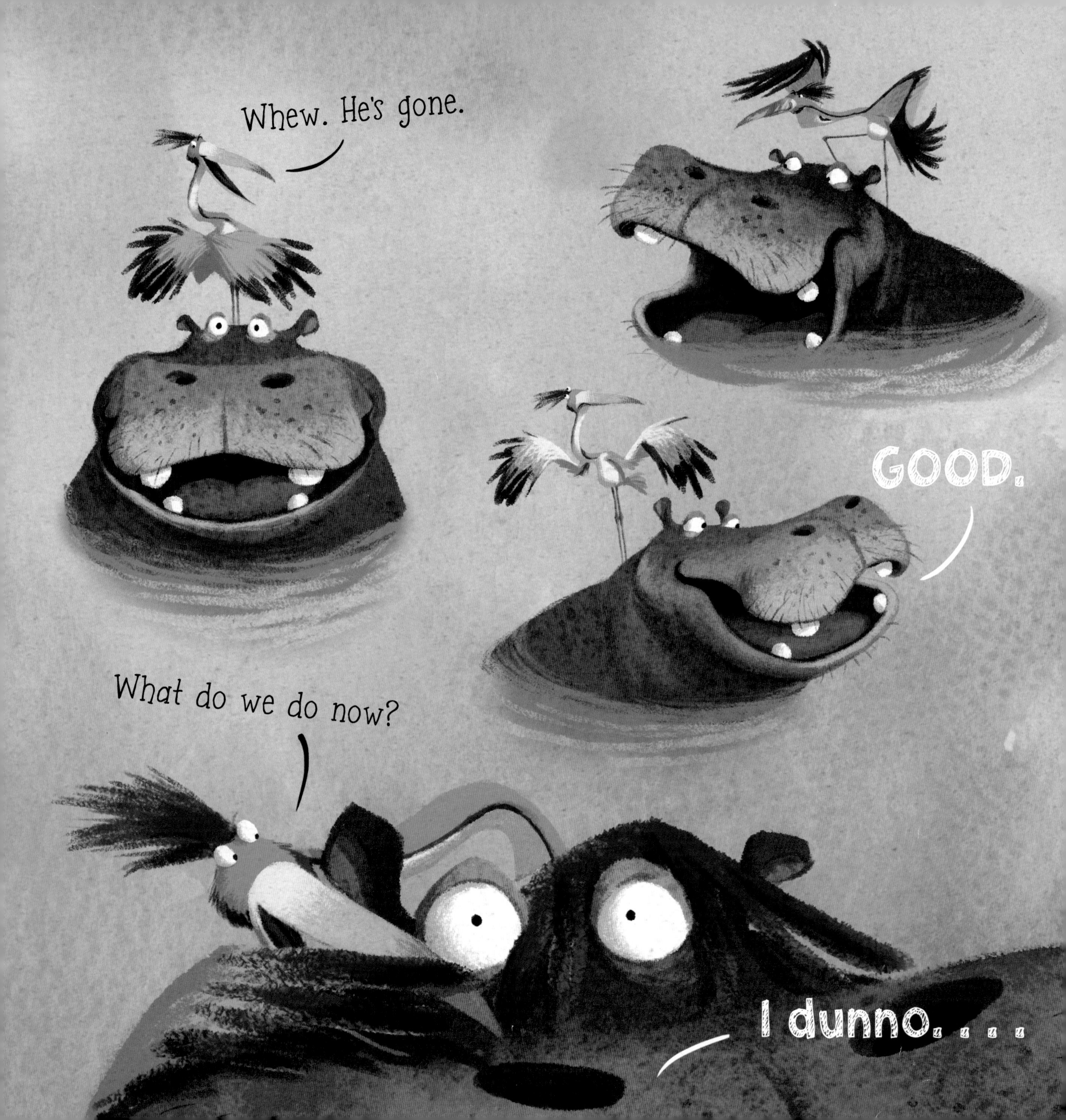
Whew. He's gone.
GOOD.
What do we do now?
I dunno. . . .

SIGH.

Well, well, well. Hello, Hippo.

ACK.
ACK.
PA-TOOEY!

Hellllp!!!

Ooooh. That sounds like an invitation to lunch.

GLIP
GLIP-GLIP
GLIP-GLIP-GLIP-GLIP-GLIP

There. You're bug-free, and I'm stuffed.
Don't we make a great team?

I told you we make a great team.

So . . . what is a hippo's favorite thing to sit on?

I dunno. A pesky bird?

His hippo-bottomus.

WHOOOOOOSH